Places

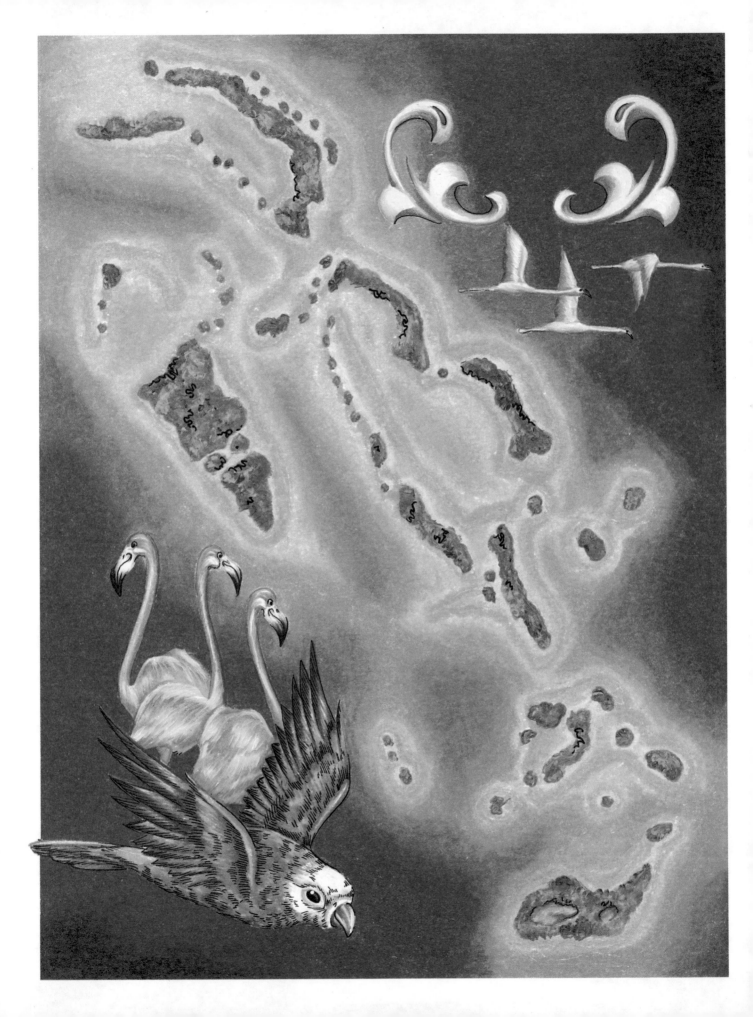

Oh No, The Pink Flamingo Turned Green!

Marilyn Sheffield
Illustrated by Katie McConnachie

MACMILLAN
CARIBBEAN

For Daniel and Louise who grew up with the magic of books.

Macmillan Education
Between Towns Road, Oxford OX4 3PP
A division of Macmillan Publishers Limited
Companies and representatives throughout the world

www.macmillan-caribbean.com

ISBN 0 333 94732 0

Text © Marilyn Sheffield 2001

Design and illustration © Macmillan Publishers Limited 2001

First published 2001

Designed by Rai & Quantrill
Illustrated by Katie McConnachie
Cover design by Rai & Quantrill
Cover illustration by Katie McConnachie

Printed and bound in Malaysia

2005 2004 2003 2002 2001
10 9 8 7 6 5 4 3 2 1

The sun was just rising when Candice awoke. It shone into her eyes and made her blink.

'Good morning, Mama,' she said. She stretched her long body and gently ruffled her beautiful pink feathers.

'Good morning, Candice. It's time for breakfast,' Mama replied.

'Mama, will you find my breakfast today?' pleaded Candice. 'Please? I'm so slow and I'm hungry.'

Candice puffed out her feathers. She looked good enough to eat. She looked fluffy, like a Candyfloss made out of sugary clouds.

Mama gave her a hug and said, 'The shrimps taste better when you find them yourself.'

Then her brother, Clive, called out, 'Stop moaning! You have to learn to feed yourself. It's not that hard, looking for shrimps.'

Clive went off to search for his breakfast. Candice was cross with her brother.

'Off you go, Candice!' said Mama. 'When you have eaten enough, you can play.'

'All right,' said Candice. She looked happier now.

'Make sure you are back at lunch time, when the sun is above your head,' said Mama.

Candice went off to search for her breakfast. Each time she spied a shrimp, it swam away.

She was just not quick enough.
'You little pests!' she said crossly.

Candice stamped her webbed foot and declared angrily, 'I'm fed up with this island. There are too many flamingos and there's not enough food.'

In fact there was enough food for everyone.

The big lake was the home of one of the biggest colonies of flamingos in the world. It was on the island of Great Inagua in the Bahamas, close to the shores of America. Around the lake grew twisting green leaf mangroves and beyond were heaps of sparkling white salt.

There was no place like it on Earth.

Candice was getting hungrier and hungrier. She could stand it no longer.

'I'm out of here!' she said aloud.

She crept away and started to fly. She had to flap her wings like crazy to lift her up into the air.

Mama watched as Candice fluttered away into the sky.

Candice looked down at the lake. She saw
pink everywhere.

'I'm right. There are too many of us.'

10

Candice flew on until she spotted some gumbo-limbo trees on a little island. 'Good!' she thought. 'There's not a single flamingo in sight. There will be plenty of breakfast for me!'

The island was the home of beautiful birds with bright blue, green, red and yellow feathers. The scent of blossom and flowers filled the air. It was Paradise!

Candice searched among the leaves on the ground. She pushed her curved beak into the flowers but she couldn't find anything that she wanted to eat.

Her eyes filled with tears.

Suddenly a yellow canary landed on a
branch of a frangipani tree above her head. He
tipped his head to one side to listen for danger.
Then he jumped onto a lower branch.

'Got you!' he sang and he flew off. A green caterpillar was hanging from his mouth.

Candice watched.

'Hmm I wonder . . .'

Candice looked closely. Lots of caterpillars were feeding on leaves. Beautiful coloured butterflies were feeding on the nectar inside pink and white petals. Bees flew by her nose and they fed from the flowers too.

'Everyone is having breakfast except me!' Candice cried in despair.

She snapped at a bright green caterpillar and swallowed it in one gulp.

'Very tasty!' she said. She was happy at last.

Candice ate until she was full. You could count the caterpillars wriggling down her narrow neck.

She chased the butterflies for a while but then she got bored and went back to Great Inagua to play with Clive on the big lake.

'Did you find any shrimps?' Clive asked.

Candice didn't say that she was full of juicy caterpillars. 'If I do, he'll tell his friends,' she thought. 'Then there'll be none left.' So she said, 'I had my breakfast somewhere else.'

'Where?' asked Clive.

'On my Secret Island,' she boasted.

For a whole week, Candice fed on bright green caterpillars on her Secret Island. She felt very pleased with herself.

Then one day she thought, 'Why am I the only flamingo here? I'll ask Mama tonight.'

But that night, when Candice got home, she was tired, so Mama sent her to bed early, saying, 'Your feathers are getting dull. You don't look very pink today. Are you ill?'

With all the fuss, Candice forgot to ask Mama her question.

On Saturday morning, Candice woke up first. She didn't want anyone else to find the juicy caterpillars so she was as quiet as a mouse.

Candice flew off without a sound.

'It's been raining very hard in the night,' thought Candice as she reached her Secret Island. There were puddles everywhere.

'I think I'll have a drink first,' she muttered to herself. She lowered her head towards the puddle. A bright green bird was looking at her!

Candice screamed out in panic. 'Ah! Help! It's me! It's my reflection! Save me, Mama! Call the doctor! Oh, no! I'm green!' she wailed.

Mama was far away on Great Inagua. She couldn't hear Candice calling for her.

Candice stood under the frangipani tree. Tears were streaming down her face. 'Now I know why there are never any flamingos here,' she sobbed.

Harold, the green parrot, watched and listened. Then he flew down and landed next to Candice. She was still crying.

'What's all this, then? We can't have tears on a summer's day,' he said.

Candice looked up through her tears. 'Can't you see I'm the wrong colour?'

'It's a lovely colour,' said Harold. 'What's wrong with green? I'm green.'

'Yes, but I'm a flamingo,' said Candice. 'Flamingos are supposed to be pink!' She started to wail again.

Harold was a majestic bird. His body, head and wings were emerald green and he had raspberry pink feathers on his chest. His long feathers for flying were edged with shiny violet blue.

He thought for a minute and said, 'I have an idea. Why don't you be a parrot for the day?'

'A parrot? Me?' said Candice.

'Just pretend. I'll look after you and it just might cheer you up,' said Harold kindly.

Candice liked the idea at once. 'Thank you, I think I will,' she said. 'I feel better already.'

The two new friends flew off together and landed where the parrots lived in a hole in a gumbo-limbo tree.

'You are a big parrot!' squeaked the baby parrot when she saw Candice standing next to her.

All the parrots laughed at the baby.

'I'm not really a parrot. I'm a flamingo gone green,' said Candice.

'Oh,' said the baby and she carried on with her flying lessons.

'Look at me! I can nearly fly.'

The baby parrot
jumped off the branch
and flapped her wings
madly but still she fell
    down
      and
        down
until Harold caught her
and carried her back to
the nest.

'Baby, you need more
practice,' he said kindly.

He called to his mother, 'We're off to play. See you later.'

Harold and Candice soared over the tree tops, chasing one another. They played hide and seek among the bushes.

'He won't find me,' thought Candice. 'Nearly everything's green, like me. Harold's green too but I can see his pink chest and the violet blue on his wings.'

Harold stopped suddenly. 'Help! Help!' his mother was calling.

In a second he was back at the nest. Candice followed close behind.

Mama Parrot was weeping. 'Baby has fallen into the lake. Please, please find her before she drowns!'

Harold squawked in dismay.

Quickly Harold flew down to the little lake. His sisters and brothers were hovering over the spot where Baby had fallen in.

'How can we rescue her?' they called. 'We can't see her anywhere!'

'Leave it to me,' said Candice, as she landed on the little lake.

It was deep. Candice was glad of her long, long legs.

'She fell in near here,' said one of the brothers.

Candice stood at the spot and put her head under the water. She looked around. There was Baby Parrot! She was lying very still ...

... on the bottom of the lake.

Candice scooped Baby up with her curved
beak and lifted her head out of the water.

She strode back to the edge of the lake and
laid the baby down.

Baby coughed and spluttered for her breath.
Water ran from her beak.

They all stood round in a circle, watching
the baby. She coughed again and again, trying
to get her breath.

Mama Parrot flew down and picked Baby
up in her beak and flew off to the nest.

Baby coughed until all the water was out of
her lungs.

'Can I fly again?' she asked. 'I feel better now!'

'Not today!' Mama Parrot said firmly.

Mama Parrot smoothed Baby's feathers. 'Tomorrow you must have more lessons,' she said. 'Harold is our best flier. He will show you how to flap your wings.'

Mama Parrot thanked Candice and then she thanked her again, and again. 'It is so lucky that you decided to be a parrot for the day. If you hadn't, Baby would have drowned!' she said.

It was time for Candice to return to the big
lake on Great Inagua Island to find her dinner.
'See you soon!' she called to her new friends.

As she flew home, Candice suddenly
remembered. 'I'm green! I've been so busy and
happy all day I forgot! What will Mama say?
I don't feel ill at all!'

Candice came to land on the edge of the big lake.

'Oh, no! Clive is playing with his friends. I didn't want him to see me just yet!'

She bravely passed the crowd of cheeky flamingos.

'Have you fallen into a can of green paint?' Clive shouted as Candice rushed to meet Mama.

His friends roared with laughter.

'Oh, Mama, I'm so glad you are here!' said Candice as she ran to her mother for comfort. 'I'm not ill, am I?'

Mama smiled and said, 'What have you been eating?'

'Caterpillars!' replied Candice. 'On my Secret Island. They were so juicy.'

'You're not ill, Candice. You've been eating the wrong food,' said her mother. 'We eat shrimps from the big lake on Great Inagua because that is what makes us so very pink. They are good for us.'

Mama gave her a big hug. Candice whispered in her ear, 'Will I stay green for ever?'

'No, of course not,' Mama replied. 'If you eat the proper food you will soon turn pink again.'

Now Clive came home. 'What happened to you, Candice? Why are you green?'

Candice told him about the caterpillars.

'Well, why didn't you ask me about the caterpillars?' said Clive. 'I'm older and I know about things like that.'

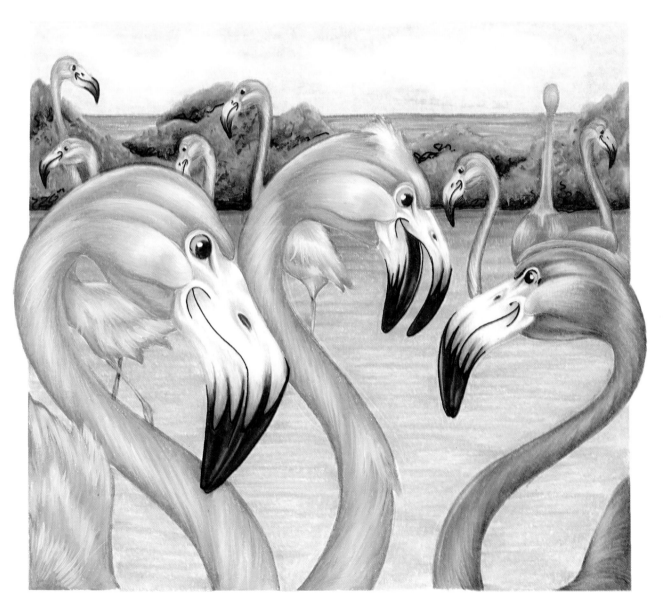

'Oh! Brothers!' thought Candice. She told Clive and Mama about Harold. She told them how she scooped Baby Parrot out of the little lake.

Clive went off and told his friends the story. They stopped making fun of Candice's green feathers. It didn't matter any more whether she was pink or green. All the flamingos were proud of her for saving a life.

In five weeks Candice had her beautiful pink feathers back. She danced and twirled on the lake. The last of her green feathers floated away.

'Hurray! I'm pink again!' she cried. 'I must show Harold!' So she flew off to his nest in the gumbo-limbo tree on her Secret Island.

Baby Parrot was flying expertly in and out of the tree tops. Harold proudly watched.

How happy they all were!